Christmas Is...

written by Sue Turner Hayes

illustrated by Kathryn Hutton

Library of Congress Catalog Card No. 86-63564
© 1987. The STANDARD PUBLISHING Company, Cincinnati, Ohio
Division of STANDEX INTERNATIONAL Corporation. Printed in U.S.A.

Christmas is just
   So exciting to me.
But sometimes I wonder
   What its meaning must be.

Christmas is full of
   Sweet smells and good sights.
Christmas is pinecones
   And bright, shiny lights.

Christmas is candy,
  All striped white and red.
Christmas is dreams
  When I'm snug in my bed.

Christmas is stockings
  That we hang up with care
By a nice cozy fire.
  Is yours hanging there?

Christmas is stories
    For young and for old,
Found in colorful books,
    They are told and retold.

Christmas is cookies
We bake every year
For family and friends,
Our loved ones so dear.

Christmas is snowmen
And cold, frosty air,
Snowballs and sled rides,
Having fun everywhere!

Christmas is presents
And gifts for us all.
Christmas is shopping
And trips to the mall.

Christmas is glitter,
   Tinsel, garland, and pine.
Christmas is windows,
   All dressed up so fine.

Christmas is holly
And bells that we ring.
Christmas is music
And carols we sing.

Christmas is family
  And loved ones who care.
Christmas is friends
  And a turkey to share.

Christmas is poinsettias,
   All pink, red, and white.
Christmas is candles,
   Shining into the night.

Christmas is parties
  And games played for fun.
When friends come to visit,
  We eat food by the ton!

Christmas is costumes
   And lines we must say,
As we practice a lot
   Getting ready for a play.

Christmas is making
   Pretty things for our tree
To hang when we decorate,
   For everyone to see.

But sometimes I wonder
　　What Christmas is about.
It's all of these things
　　But I really do doubt . . .

That Christmas is gifts
  And a wreath on the door.
I think that Christmas
  Must mean so much more.

Christmas is warm,
   Although there is snow.
Christmas goes with me
   Wherever I go.

Christmas is not just
   What I see at the mall,
Or just toys or presents,
   Or snowflakes that fall.

It's not in the goodies
Meant only for me,
Or in glitter and tinsel,
Or under the tree.

Christmas is not
    What I put on my table.
Christmas is a night
    In a small, humble stable.

Christmas is angels
And tidings of joy.
Christmas is shepherds
And a newborn baby boy.

Christmas is love,
   God's love for me.
Christmas is Jesus,
   And His birthday, you see.